Happy Birthday, Royal Baby!

by Martha Mumford

illustrated by
Ada Grey

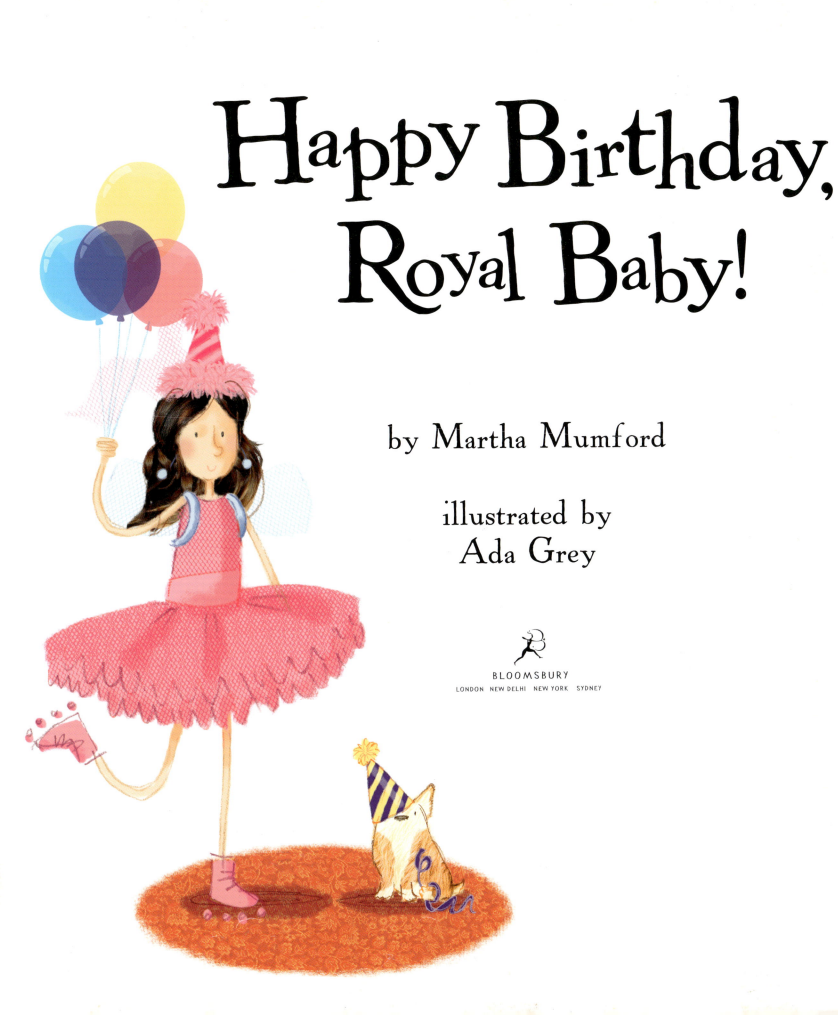

BLOOMSBURY
LONDON NEW DELHI NEW YORK SYDNEY

The Royal Palace was awash with activity.
It was the Royal Baby's first birthday.

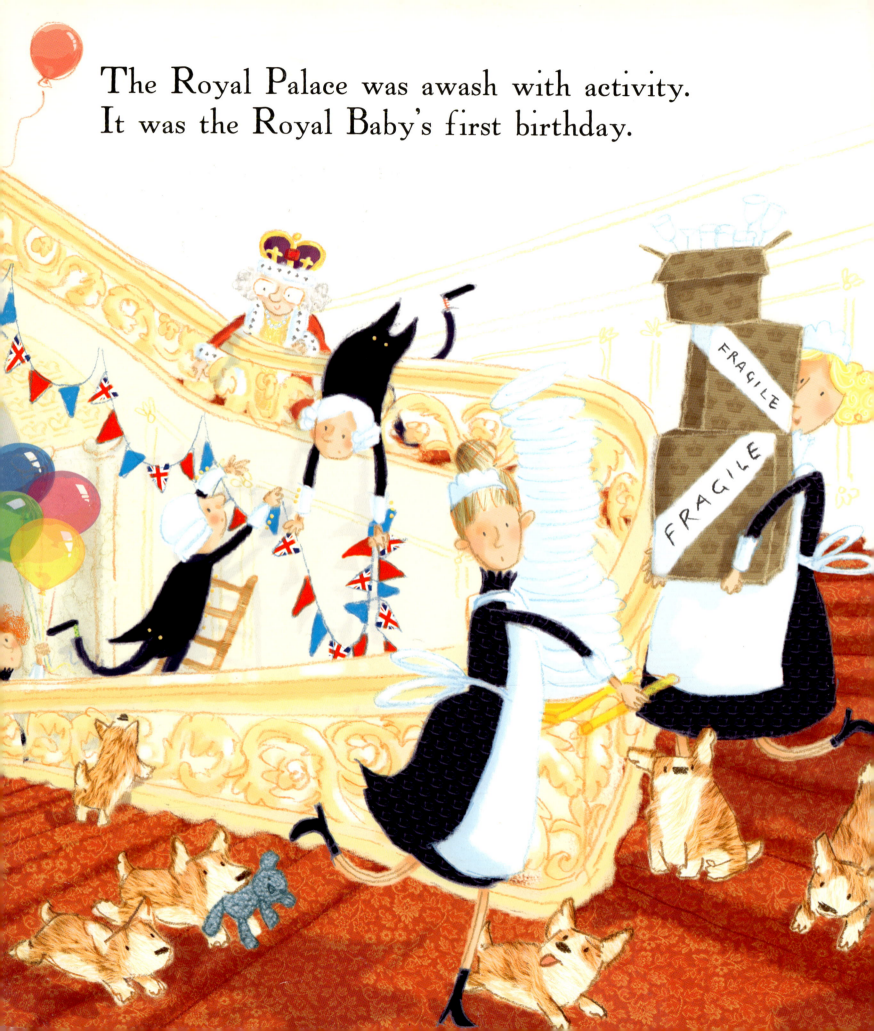

"Everything needs to be perfect for the Royal Baby's celebrations," bustled the young prince's auntie.

In the palace kitchen, the head cook was busy making the biggest cake you have ever seen.

50 eggs
1000g sugar
1000g flour
Butter - lots!
Icing - lots & lots!

"Don't forget the jam," said the prince's auntie. "The Royal Baby LOVES jam!"

In the banqueting hall, the royal
balloon blower was busy blowing up a
mountain of balloons – all by himself!

"More puff! More puff!" said the prince's grandma. "You've still got more than a hundred to go — and don't forget the dinosaur-shaped ones. The Royal Baby LOVES dinosaurs!"

In the palace gardens, the royal gardener was mowing the lawns, trimming the hedges and spraying the royal roses with perfume.

"Don't forget the bouncy castle," said the prince's grandad. "The Royal Baby LOVES bouncing!"

Meanwhile, in the music hall, the royal conductor was directing the royal orchestra whilst the royal choir practised scales.

Doh, rae, mee . . .

"Don't forget the speakers," shouted the prince's uncle. The Royal Baby LOVES music!"

Finally, it was time for the party to begin.
Guests arrived from near and far,
carrying gifts of all shapes and sizes.

There were games of Pin the Tail on the Corgi,

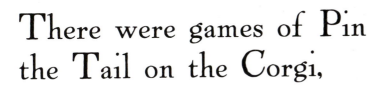

Musical Thrones,

and a particularly spectacular (and very long) game of Pass the Peacock.

Everyone was having a wonderful time —
everyone, that is, except the Royal Baby.

Waaaaaaah!

Waaaaaaah!

Waaaaaaah!

The Royal Baby
was not happy at all.

"Whatever is the matter with him?"
sighed the Duchess.
"I've no idea," said the Duke. "I thought
we'd remembered all the things he loves."

 "Presents, silly!" shouted the prince's
grandad. "One always relishes the
present-opening on one's birthday — you
haven't helped him open his presents."

And you have never seen a bigger pile of presents!
The Duke and Duchess set to work, helping
the prince tear off the wrapping paper.

There were toys that walked, toys that talked;
toys that whizzed and toys that fizzed;
tall toys, small toys;
toys that beeped, toys that squeaked;
flashing toys, bashing toys . . .

. . . all the toys you could imagine, and much more besides. But . . . still the prince cried.

Waaaaaaah!
Waaaaaaah!
Waaaaaaah!

"Oh dear," sighed the Queen. "I suppose you'd better leave this to me."

Minutes later, the Queen's private jet
flew overhead. Its vapour trail wrote a
message in the sky:

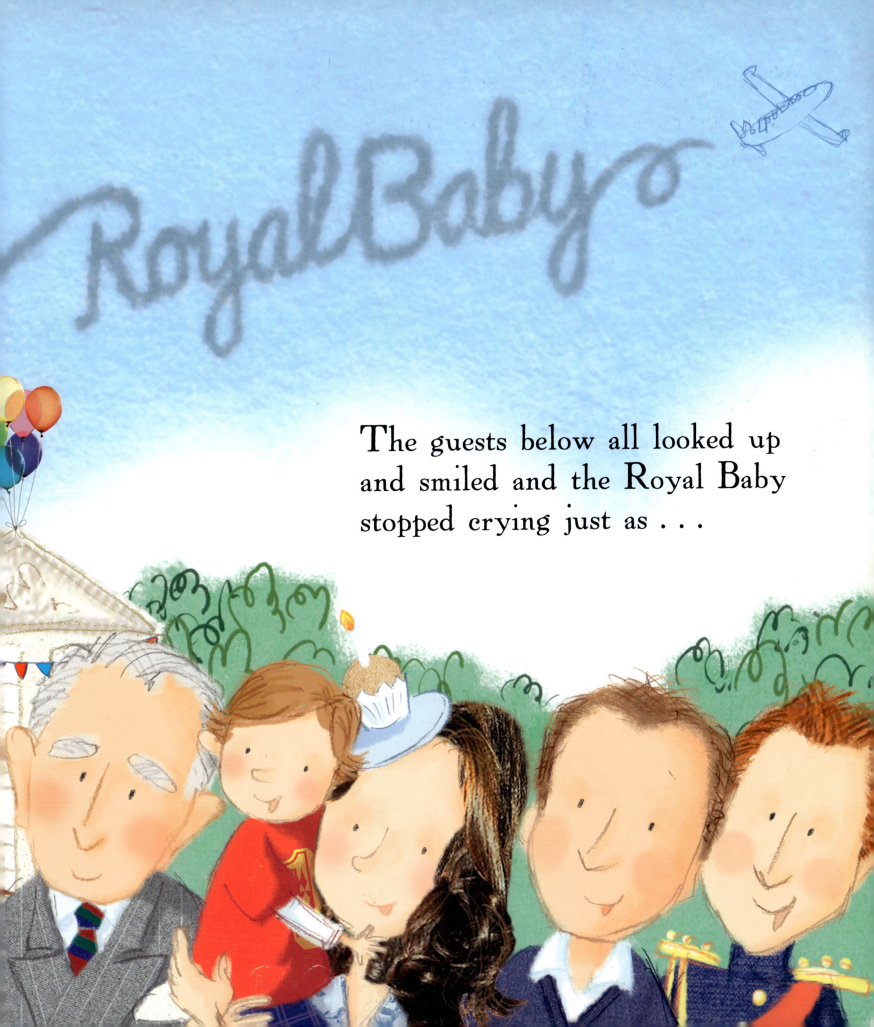

The guests below all looked up
and smiled and the Royal Baby
stopped crying just as . . .

GERONIMO!

The Queen parachuted to the ground with a birthday present strapped to her front.

"Happy birthday, my little darling!" she said, handing over the present. The Royal Baby tore off the wrapping paper and found a cardboard box.

"What's inside?" whispered the Duchess.
"Nothing," said the Queen.
"Nothing?" said the Duke, astonished.
"Nothing!" said the Queen. "Now, just be quiet and watch."

The Royal Baby peered into the empty box,
looked up at the Queen and . . . with that, he
bounced up and down excitedly, grabbed his
toy dinosaur and clambered into the box.

"Happy Birthday, to you,

Happy Birthday, to you,

Happy Birthday,
Royal Baby!

Happy Birthday, to you!"

The Royal Baby blew out his candle.
"Hip, hip, hooray!" everyone cried.
Then it was slices of cake all around
and an especially jammy slice for
the very happy Royal Baby.

"So we did get it right, after all," laughed the Duke. "Look! He loves jam, dinosaurs, music and bouncing!"

"And cardboard boxes too," giggled the Duchess.

And they were right
– the Royal Baby was
having the most fun ever.

And later, much later, when the Royal Baby was tucked up and fast asleep, the grown-ups had the most fun ever too!

Happy Birthday, Royal Baby!

For Fiz and Kayt,
with thanks for all the hard work – MM

For Mum and Dad – AG

Bloomsbury Publishing, London, New Delhi, New York and Sydney

First published in Great Britain in 2014 by Bloomsbury Publishing Plc
50 Bedford Square, London, WC1B 3DP

A CIP catalogue record for this book is available from the British Library

ISBN 978 1 4088 5482 2 (PB)

ISBN 978 1 4088 5481 5 (eBook)

Printed and bound in Italy by L.E.G.O SpA

1 3 5 7 9 10 8 6 4 2

All papers used by Bloomsbury Publishing are natural, recyclable products made
from wood grown in well-managed forests. The manufacturing processes conform
to the environmental regulations of the country of origin

www.bloomsbury.com
BLOOMSBURY is a registered trademark of Bloomsbury Publishing Plc